The Wheels

SCHOOL
BUS
STOP

illustrated by **Bari Weissman**

GT
PUBLISHING

NEW YORK

The wheels on the bus go round and round,
round and round,
round and round.
The wheels on the bus go round and round,
all around the town.

The wipers on the bus go swish, swish, swish,
swish, swish, swish,
swish, swish, swish.
The wipers on the bus go swish, swish, swish,
all around the town,

The driver on the bus goes "Move on back!"
"Move on back!"
"Move on back!"
The driver on the bus goes "Move on back!"
all around the town.

The kids on the bus go up and down,
up and down,
up and down.
The kids on the bus go up and down,
all around the town.

The horn on the bus goes beep, beep, beep!
Beep, beep, beep!
Beep, beep, beep!
The horn on the bus goes beep, beep, beep!
all around the town.

The girls on the bus go "Hee, hee, hee!"
"Hee, hee, hee!"
"Hee, hee, hee!"
The girls on the bus go "Hee, hee, hee!"
all around the town.

The dog on the bus goes yip, yip, yip,
yip, yip, yip,
yip, yip, yip.
The dog on the bus goes yip, yip, yip,
all around the town.

The ball on the bus goes bounce, bounce, bounce,
bounce, bounce, bounce,
bounce, bounce, bounce.
The ball on the bus goes bounce, bounce, bounce,
all around the town.

The frog on the bus goes hop, hop, hop,
hop, hop, hop,
hop, hop, hop.
The frog on the bus goes hop, hop, hop,
all around the town.

The boys on the bus go "Ha, ha, ha!"
"Ha, ha, ha!"
"Ha, ha, ha!"
The boys on the bus go "Ha, ha, ha!"
all around the town.

The driver on the bus goes "Here we are,"
"Here we are,"
"Here we are."
The driver on the bus goes "Here we are,"
all around the town.

**The wheels on the bus go round and round,
all around the town.**